MARVEL STUDIOS

THOR

MARVEL STUDIOS

THOR

A NOVEL BASED ON THE MAJOR MOTION PICTURE

Adapted by Elizabeth Rudnick

Based on the screenplay by Ashley Edward Miller & Zack Stentz and Don Payne

Story by J. Michael Straczynski and Mark Protosevich

NEW YORK

Published by Marvel Press, an imprint of Disney Publishing Worldwide. No part of this book may be reproduced or transmitted in any form or by any means, electronic or mechanical, including photocopying, recording, or by any information storage and retrieval system, without written permission from the publisher. For information address Marvel Press, 114 Fifth Avenue, New York, New York 10011-5690.

Printed in the United States of America

First Edition

1 3 5 7 9 10 8 6 4 2

J689-1817-1-11046

ISBN 978-1-4231-4311-6

CONTENTS

PROLOGUE

THEY'VE ALWAYS ASKED QUESTIONS— this race called man, on this planet called Earth. Passionately longing to know how they are connected to the heavens. In ages past, they looked to us as gods, for indeed so many times we saved them from calamity. We tried to show them how their world was but one of the Nine Realms of the cosmos, linked to all others by the branches of Yggdrasil . . . the World Tree. Nine Realms in a universe of wonder, beauty, and terror which they barely comprehended.

But for all their thirst for knowledge, they let our knowledge, they let our lessons, fall into myth and dream.

The mighty Thor. Where did he—the one whom the humans call the God of Thunder—come from? He came from us, the proudest warriors the worlds have ever seen. He came from this—the greatest realm the universe has ever known.

Thor came from . . . Asgard.

And these are his tales. . . .

THE ALLFATHER'S FEAR

Odin Allfather did not act without thought. Now, as the sun shone over Asgard and the buildings were illuminated by its rays, gleaming like gold, he thought long and hard. At the realm's edge, the darkness of the cosmos spread out like a calm sea. Asgard was at peace, and all was ready for the momentous events to come.

Standing in his chambers, Odin stared out at the realm he had ruled for so many years. Despite the beauty before him, his mind was troubled and his expression drawn with worry and tension.

As Allfather, Odin had battled great beasts, invaded foreign realms, destroyed strong enemies, and kept the realm of Asgard safe and peaceful.

He had lost his brothers and father to war. For thousands upon thousands of years, he had carried the burden of his crown alone. It had wearied him at times, energized him at others. When he had married his wife, Frigga, the burden had lifted as she was a strong partner and had a helpful ear. And with the birth of his first son, Thor, Odin had felt hopeful that one day he would be able to pass along his crown to a worthy successor and find the peace he so rightly deserved.

Now that day had finally come. For today, Thor would become king.

Yet Odin did not feel a sense of relief.

With a deep sigh, he turned from the wide doorway that led out to his chamber balcony. Behind him the two giant statues of his fallen brothers that stood outside the palace framed his tired body, dwarfing him, while at the same time hinting at his great might and heritage. He was not yet dressed for the evening but still in the golden robes that would soon be exchanged for his ceremonial gear. But his hair was combed and his face freshly shaved. Odin's shoulder-length hair was no longer the rich brown of his youth, but the gray suited him and he still had the bearing of a great warrior and powerful leader.

Queen Frigga sat at her vanity, putting on her jewelry. In the reflection, she saw her husband turn and come back into the center of the room. His blue eyes were dark with worry, and she felt a now long-familiar rush of love. She had married a warrior but knew him as so much more than that. He did not rule lightly. Everything he had done and everything he would do was the result of great reflection. He had seen the results of battles that had not been thought out and had lost too many warriors to unnecessary violence. And so she knew that he had thought long and hard about this day.

While some argued that Thor should have assumed the throne years ago, Odin had seen the benefit in waiting. He wanted his son to follow in his footsteps and the footsteps of his father before him—to keep Asgard safe and free of war. Yet Thor was not his father. He was impulsive and hotheaded. He still had much to learn about the value of patience. Alas, Odin had no more time left to teach. He was growing weaker by the day. Soon, he would need to enter the Odinsleep, during which he would be unable to rule, his body in a state of suspended animation while he used the powerful Odinforce to rejuvenate.

Feeling his wife's gaze on him, Odin looked up and smiled, the corners of his eyes crinkling. She continued to amaze him. Her beauty was beyond compare, and while servants rushed about in preparation below, she sat calmly, her back straight and her head high. Now, more than ever, he needed her strength.

"Do you think he's ready?" Odin asked, his voice deep with emotion.

She looked at him and nodded slowly. "Thor has his father's wisdom," she said, knowing that was what he needed to hear. But Odin's expression remained worried so she added, "He won't be alone. Loki will be at his side to give him counsel."

Standing up, she approached her husband. Loki, their youngest son, was a source of tension between them. Odin had always favored Thor because Thor was a warrior, just like himself, but Loki was not, and so his youngest formed a closer bond with Queen Frigga. But in a way, that had been a good balance. Loki was Thor's opposite— quiet, thoughtful, and content to stay in the shadows. She hoped that Odin would see the benefit of having the brothers side-by-side.

He reached out a hand, about to caress her cheek. But he stopped suddenly.

Odin's hand was shaking. The Allfather stood staring at it with fierce concentration, as though willing it to stop. "If we only had more time," Odin said when his hand finally stopped shaking. "I can fight it a little longer. . . ."

Frigga held up a hand. "No! You've put it off too long!" she said harshly. Then her expression softened. "I worry for you."

Odin cocked his head, a playful smile tugging at his lips. "I've destroyed demons and monsters, devastated whole worlds, laid waste to mighty kingdoms, and still you worry for me?"

"Always," Frigga answered truthfully. She knew what he was capable of, but she still feared that Thor's new role would be Odin's undoing.

But she didn't have to worry. Her words had reassured her husband as they always did, and now, for better or worse, he was ready to pass on the throne to his eldest son.

～≈≈～

A short while later, a horn sounded throughout the palace. Inside the throne room, Asgardians had gathered to bid farewell to their current king and welcome their new king. Ceremonial banners fluttered from the high ceilings while attendants handed out golden goblets full of sweet drinks to the beautifully dressed guests. There was a festive air to the room as people chatted softly to each other and waited with eager anticipation for the arrival of the royal family.

At the front of the room, Thor's best friends and fellow warriors, Volstagg, Fandral, Hogun, and the Lady Sif, stood at attention while members of the palace guard lined up in formation. Then Frigga entered the room and walked down the long aisle, Loki by her side. Her hair cascaded over her shoulders and down her back in ringlets that matched her golden gown. In honor of the event, Loki wore his horned helmet and signature green cape. When they had made their way to the front of the room, another horn sounded and the guards stepped aside. There was an audible gasp.

Odin sat atop his golden throne. On his head he wore a large helmet and in his hand he gripped the mighty spear Gungnir.

Looking out over the room, Odin sighed deeply. Even after ruling for tens of thousands of years, it felt like only a day ago that his father had crowned him in a ceremony similar to this one. He wondered now if his father had had the same doubts he was having about Thor. Did he regret having to step aside for the younger generation to take over? Odin thought. Was I as impulsive then as Thor is now? Does that mean that he, too, will grow into a wise king in time?

Odin's thoughts were interrupted by another gasp from the crowd. Then the room erupted in applause. The mighty Thor had arrived.

Thor raised Mjolnir, the hammer that only he could lift, high over his head and soaked in the adoration. It was as if he had harnessed the powers of the storm to make his entrance all the more spectacular. His body was covered in battle armor with large metal disks on the front chest plate. His winged helmet sat on his head, and his long red cape flowed behind him. While moments ago, everyone had believed Odin to be the most powerful ruler they would ever have, the appearance of Thor made them believe otherwise. Standing there, he looked every inch a king.

When the cheering faded, Thor finally strode up the long aisle, a smug smile on his face. Clearly the concerns of his father did not trouble Thor. He felt more than ready to rule Asgard. He had watched his father do it for years, and he thought it was time for a fresh start. He had proven himself to be one of the finest warriors the realm had ever seen. Now he would prove himself to be one of its finest kings.

As Odin watched his son walk toward him, the gravity of the situation hit the Allfather hard. Thor had grown into a fine young man. And now, Odin's brash and oftentimes irresponsible son was about to take the throne as the new ruler of

Asgard. Yet Odin could still vividly remember when Thor was just a boy, learning how to hold a sword for the first time. Or when he was first able to wield Mjolnir. How the hammer, which now looked small in his large hands, had nearly toppled Thor!

Odin smiled now, thinking back on that day. Learning to be king would be like learning to ride a horse. Thor wouldn't like having to go slowly and he would fall a few times, but his difficulties would serve to teach him some valuable lessons. Or so Odin hoped. He could only be grateful that the realm was at peace and had been for a long time. There was no doubt Thor was a good warrior—but a warrior king? That was another story. That was something he had yet to learn.

Finally, Thor arrived in front of his father. He nodded at his mother and brother and friends and then kneeled, bowed his head, and waited. A hush fell over the crowd as they, too, waited.

"A new day has come for a new king to wield his own weapon," Odin began, his deep voice echoing through the room. "Today, I entrust you with the sacred throne of Asgard. Responsibility, duty, honor. They are essential to every soldier and every king." As the Allfather spoke, Thor raised his eyes. Odin willed the words to impact his son, to get through to him. For after this day, he would be on his own.

Odin continued, speaking the words that had been spoken to him so many years before. He was at the very end of his speech when he felt it—a chill that cut through the room and caused people to shiver uncertainly. Odin's heart began to race. He had felt this chill before—on Jotunheim. Asgard had waged a long and fierce war with the Ice Realm. But a truce had been made years ago. There was no reason for Odin to think Jotuns would be in Asgard. Still . . .

Shaking off the feeling of dread, Odin continued. He was just about to say the final words that would make Thor king when the banners hanging from the ceiling suddenly iced over.

There was no denying it. "Frost Giants," Odin whispered.

≈≈≈

Before Odin could stop him, Thor raced out of the room, his red cape flying behind him and Mjolnir clutched in his hand.

Turning, Odin ordered the guards to be on alert and then followed the chill out of the room. He had a very good idea about what the Frost Giants were after—the Casket of Ancient Winters. The Casket enabled anyone who held it to create a never-ending winter. Laufey, the Jotun king, had wanted to use the Casket to turn all the realms into frozen ice lands that he could rule. Years earlier, Odin had taken the Casket in order to insure it would never be misused. For the safety of all Nine Realms, he had it placed in the Vault. The large, cavernous space was deep below the palace and housed the realm's greatest threats. Although it was guarded at all times, someone must have gotten in.

When he arrived at the Vault, his assumptions were proven true. He found Thor staring at the remains of a great battle. Two Asgardian sentries lay on the floor, frozen solid. Towering above them stood the Destroyer, Odin's deadliest weapon. This menacing creature was nothing but armor filled with mystical Odinforce. When a threat to Odin or Asgard was felt, the Destroyer would awaken and the Odinforce would burn bright, laying waste to anyone or anything that got in its way.

Now, the Destroyer held the Casket of Ancient Winters in its hands.

❧❦❧

Thor turned, and his eyes met his father's. While Odin's eyes were troubled and resigned,

Thor's blazed with unabashed fury. This was an act of war! While up above, a roomful of the most important people in the Nine Realms had been celebrating, the Vault had been broken into and two sentries killed. All of Asgard could be at risk. Something had to be done.

Odin watched as various emotions played over his son's face. He knew Thor was angry and that he wanted revenge. A part of him wanted that, too. If Laufey had sent the Frost Giants, it meant that he no longer valued the truce. On the other hand, if Laufey *hadn't* sent them and the rogue Jotuns had acted on their own, then Odin might be starting an unnecessary war by retaliating.

"The Jotuns must pay for what they've done!" Thor shouted, interrupting his father's thoughts.

The king shook his head sadly. He had hoped Thor would think rationally about the consequences. "I have a truce with Laufey," Odin reminded Thor. "What action would you take?"

Thor puffed out his chest. He knew exactly what he would do. "March into Jotunheim as you once did and teach them a lesson."

"The Casket of Ancient Winters belonged to the Jotuns. They believe it's their birthright," Odin said, his voice heavy.

The two men stood facing each other, one old, one young, both determined. Odin would not let Thor travel to Jotunheim. It would solve nothing and most certainly send the realms into war. This was not the time for it. Thor had not yet been named king, and Odin was too old to face a lengthy battle.

The room seemed to fill with tension. The Casket, safely back on its pedestal, glowed with an unnatural blue light, casting shadows over the men's faces. Finally, Thor had had enough. His father was too old and too set in his ways. This very action was why he should have been named king long ago. He said as much and watched his father's eyes grow sad.

Odin forbade him from going to Jotunheim and saw Thor's eyes harden. Turning on his heels, the mighty Thor left the Vault, defeated by his own father.

Odin felt his limbs begin to shake. He was uneasy and unsure about Agsard's future and about his own health—and that frightened him.

～≈≈≈≈≈～

Since their fight the night before, Odin had not seen his eldest son. He had heard his muffled shouts in the banquet hall as Thor told friends what had happened, but Odin had heard nothing since. Frigga had tried to assure him that Thor's temper would ease and this would blow over, but Odin knew better.

Just then, a guard rushed over to him and told him news of Thor's journey into Jotunheim. Odin felt a deep well of fury rise up within him. Thor had deliberately disobeyed his orders.

"Tell the barn master to have Sleipnir saddled and my battle gear readied immediately," he ordered the guard. It looked like Odin would be making one more trip to the icy realm of Jotunheim.

Moments later, Odin raced across the Rainbow Bridge astride his eight-legged steed. Odin was right to worry. Thor—along with Loki, the Warriors Three, and Lady Sif—had broken the truce and entered Jotunheim, thereby endangering them all.

The wind whipped Odin's face, but he didn't notice. His anger had been replaced by fear. Jotunheim was nothing but an icy wasteland now. Its surface cracked and broke apart constantly, leaving less and less of the realm. And the Frost Giants were fierce warriors with the ability to create weapons made of ice that were as sharp as the finest Asgardian blades. He did not want to think about what Thor and his band of five would be going through right now. He urged his horse to go faster.

Odin felt the familiar sense of his body being tugged and pulled out of proportion and then a sudden rush as all his molecules came crashing back together. A moment later there was a great ripping sound and a hole opened up in front of him. Beyond it he could make out the white ice of Jotunheim—and Thor. His son and the other warriors were completely surrounded by Frost Giants!

Landing, Sleipnir reared up, his powerful front legs pawing the air. Odin's arrival stopped everyone in their tracks, giving him the chance to race over to Laufey. Pulling aside the Jotun king, he whispered, "You and I can stop this before there's further bloodshed."

Laufey stared at the Asgardian king with hate burning in his eyes. His blue skin was aged and wrinkled, but there was still pride in his stance. He shook his head. "Your boy sought this out," Laufey replied. "He'll get what he came for—war and death."

The Jotun king signaled to his giants, and they began to move forward. Looking over at his son, Odin saw that he looked beaten and worn, as did the others. One of the warriors had a gaping shoulder wound and another had a blackened, frostbitten arm. They did not stand a chance against the giants, not even with the king's added strength.

Sighing, he knew what must be done. Odin raised his mighty spear Gungnir high over his head and slammed it down into the ice. The massive impact knocked back the advancing Frost Giants and caused the ice to break and crack. Odin then quickly called upon the Bifrost. Another hole ripped the sky, and before Laufey or the other Frost Giants could react, Odin pulled himself and the other Asgardians up and out of Jotunheim.

They were safe.

But now Odin would have to deal with Thor.

⁓⁓

As soon as they arrived back in the Observatory, Odin sent Lady Sif and the Warriors Three back to the palace. What Odin had to say must only be said to family. Turning to his eldest son, he looked for any sign that Thor was sorry for what he had done. A sign that he knew his actions were those of a bold and arrogant young man not yet ready to rule. But Odin saw none, even when he told Thor he'd been wrong for going to Jotunheim and that he had almost put an end to a peace that had lasted for years. Even then, Thor just stood there, defiant as always.

"You're a vain, greedy, cruel boy," Odin said finally, the words hot on his tongue.

"And you are an old man and a fool!" Thor shouted back.

Odin felt a great weariness wash over him. The trip through the Bifrost had taken more energy than he had left to give, and his son's words stabbed at him. "Yes," he said, his voice bitter. "I was a fool to think you were ready."

Odin Allfather did not act without thought. And he had thought through the past days' events quite thoroughly. He knew what he had to do, even if it meant losing his son forever. Thor needed to learn to be a true king. He needed to learn compassion and humility and patience, and he couldn't do that here on Asgard.

Thor needed to be stripped of his godly powers and sent to a realm where he would bleed and hurt like a mortal. He had to learn to put the needs of others before his own so that he would be able to do the same for his people. There was no other choice. Thor needed to be sent to Midgard. He needed to be sent to Earth.

Stepping forward, Odin went to stand in front of the panel that controlled the Bifrost. He plunged his spear into the device, and the Observatory began to hum with energy. Turning, he walked over toward his eldest son as his youngest looked on.

"You are unworthy of this realm," he said, ripping a disk off Thor's chest armor.

"Unworthy of your title . . ." He ripped away his cloak.

"Unworthy of the loved ones you've betrayed." Odin's voice cracked with emotion as he went on. "I hereby take from you your powers." He held out a hand and Mjolnir flew into it.

Thor's eyes grew wide as the reality of the situation began to hit him. But his father wasn't finished. "In the name of my father," Odin continued, "and of his father before . . .

"I CAST YOU OUT!" Odin finished. The Bifrost glowed strong, and in one swift move Odin pushed Thor through the portal. In moments, his son was gone from view.

Then, looking down at the hammer he still held, Odin quietly added, "Whosoever holds this hammer, if he be worthy, shall possess the power of Thor." With the last of his strength, he threw the hammer into the portal and watched it disappear.

A violent shaking then overtook Odin. Time was running out, and there was much at stake. Would Asgard once again be at war with Jotunheim? Would Thor ever learn his lesson and find his way back home? Would father and son ever reconcile?

And most pressing, with Thor gone and Odin sleeping, who would rule the realm?

Odin Allfather did not act without thought. But as the Odinsleep consumed him, he feared his thoughtful actions this time might mean the very end of Asgard. . . .

A GROWING CHILL

In a few short minutes, the mighty Thor would succeed his father and become the new king of Asgard. All attention would be on him, just as he liked it. No one would notice Thor's younger brother. No one would notice Loki, the Trickster. And that's just the way Loki liked it.

Loki paused behind thick curtains as he made his way toward the elaborate Asgardian throne room. For now it was quiet, with no sign of the large crowds of Asgardians that would soon fill the space. It was just Loki. On his head he wore his great helmet, its two horns rising up and then curving like a ram's. He was dressed in his finest clothes and wore his signature green cape. He soaked in the silence and for a moment imagined that it was he who would walk down the aisle to kneel in front of Odin and ascend to the throne of Asgard. He imagined thunderous applause and saw his mother glowing with pride as he stood, ready to rule.

Hearing the sound of loud footsteps, he shook off the fantasy and turned. His brother was striding down the long hall toward him. Towering over even the tallest of Asgardians, his chest broad and his shoulders straight, Thor held Mjolnir in his hand as he walked, and his long red cape flowed out behind him. Even Thor's helmet seemed more powerful than Loki's, its wings catching rays of sun and looking perfect atop his golden locks.

"Nervous, brother?" Loki said when Thor came to a stop in front of him. His eyes were teasing. He knew that Thor never got nervous.

"How do I look?" Thor asked, ignoring his brother's question. He adjusted his red cape and ran a hand over his armor. He may not have been nervous, but he did want to make sure that he looked the part. He had been waiting for this day for years. Nothing could spoil it for him now.

"Like a king," Loki answered, his eyes flashing.

Thor gave him a quizzical look. Loki's answer had been honest, but his tone had held a hint of something he couldn't quite read. Jealousy? Anger? Envy? His younger brother had always been something of a mystery to him. While Thor had been eager to spread his wings, fight in battles, and go off on grand adventures, Loki had always been more hesitant. True, he had Thor's back, but it was often only out of necessity. So why would Loki be jealous now? He couldn't want the throne for himself, could he?

As if sensing Thor's hesitation, Loki smiled, erasing the fire in his eyes and replacing it with affection. Then, to Thor's amusement, he turned to a servant passing by with a goblet full of wine. The wine morphed into a group of writhing eels that slithered up the servant's hand and arm. The servant let out a scream and dropped the goblet, which clattered to the ground. Instantly, the eels disappeared and were replaced by spilled wine. Thor laughed, reassured. Loki was a trickster and a magician. He did not want to be king.

Then Loki spoke, confirming Thor's thoughts. "I've looked forward to this day as long as you have," he said, his voice serious. "You're my brother and my friend. Sometimes I'm envious, but never doubt I love you."

Suddenly, a horn blasted. It was time for the ceremony to begin.

❦

After leaving so Thor could prepare for his entrance, Loki made his way to the front of the throne room. The Warriors Three—Volstagg, Fandral, and Hogun—were already at their places of honor, along with Lady Sif. The four were Thor's lifelong friends. Together, they had gone on many adventures in which Loki had only taken a reluctant part.

The room had grown crowded and was filled with muffled conversation as everybody eagerly awaited Thor's arrival. But first, Odin appeared, seated on his golden throne, spear in hand. His expression showed pride—and perhaps a hint of sadness—as he looked out over the room. Loki felt a pang, wondering if Odin had ever looked that way at him. Shaking off the thought, he focused on the door again.

"Where is he?" Loki heard Volstagg mutter. "I'm famished. And Odin will not be happy with the delay."

Turning, Loki gave him a look. The huge warrior was *always* hungry. "I wouldn't worry," he said softly. "Father will forgive him. He always does."

Then, as if in response to Loki's words, the room erupted in applause. Standing at the opposite end of the throne room holding his hammer high above his head was Loki's brother and the future king of Asgard, the mighty Thor.

As Thor kneeled in front of Odin, Loki watched, his expression unreadable. Today, everything would change. For better or worse, he could not tell. Would Thor be a good king? A wise king? Or would he be a rash and foolish one? There were times Loki doubted that Thor was ready—he didn't listen and he was quick to judge. Would Asgard benefit from such a leader? Watching him now, as Odin spoke the words his own father had spoken to him thousands of years before, Loki had to admit Thor looked like a king.

Odin had just gotten to the final part of the ceremony when a chill filled the room. Loki shivered and rubbed his arms. Trying to ignore the feeling, Loki turned his attention back to Odin, who hadn't stopped. But then, the banners that hung from the high ceilings suddenly crackled and iced over.

Up on his throne, Odin's expression grew serious. He seemed to know exactly what was causing this strange behavior. "Frost Giants," Loki heard him hiss.

And then, as he and everyone else watched in shock, Thor stood up and ran from the room. The Warriors Three and Lady Sif followed. Sighing, Odin went after them.

Loki turned and looked at his mother. "What is going on?" he asked.

"I have no idea," Frigga answered. "But I suggest you go and find out."

⁂

Loki found the answer in the palace's Vault. The large underground chamber held all of Asgard's most dangerous weapons, and its spoils of war. It was not a place Loki visited as it was heavily guarded, cold, dark, and home to the Destroyer. The large armored creature was Odin's greatest weapon. Filled with Odinforce, it could destroy anything that got in its way.

And apparently, something had gotten in its way.

When Loki arrived, he found his brother and father standing among the remains of a great battle. Thor's body was tense and his eyes were filled with rage as he looked upon the dead bodies of two Asgardians.

"They must pay for what they've done!" Loki heard him say to Odin.

Odin looked defeated. The Frost Giants of Jotunheim, who were led by King Laufey, were strong warriors and fierce enemies. A truce had ended the war between Odin and Laufey, but Odin had not left anything to chance. He had taken Laufey's greatest weapon—the Casket of Ancient Winters—and put it in the Vault, where it had remained safe. Until today.

Raising his eyes from the floor, Odin looked at his eldest son. "I have a truce with Laufey," he said. "What action would you take?"

"March into Jotunheim as you once did and teach them a lesson!" Thor answered quickly.

Loki heard his father sigh. That was not the answer Odin had wanted to hear. If Thor were to do that, it would cause an all-out war. When Loki had been musing on his brother's ability to lead earlier, he had never imagined that the day would come so soon. Yet Thor had not been made king—and Odin still remained ruler of Asgard. It was up to him to make the decision.

Suddenly, Loki felt his father's gaze on him. The Allfather then turned his attention to Lady Sif and the Warriors Three. "Leave, now," Odin ordered them. "I will have words with my son."

As the Warriors left, Loki saw the anger and disappointment in his father's eyes. Thor's actions would plunge Asgard into a full-scale war. Odin would not tolerate such a thing, but Thor disagreed. And that's when the yelling started.

Loki knew his father had been clear: Thor was not to act upon the Jotuns. But he also knew that his brother would not accept that command. Thor was not one to wait patiently. Later, when Loki entered the banquet hall, he was not surprised to find Thor raging.

His brother was pacing up and down, his long strides echoing like thunder off the walls. The Warriors Three and Lady Sif had just entered the room, their faces worried, when suddenly Thor walked over to the long table that had been set for his celebration dinner. He flipped it over as though it weighed no more than a feather. Food and drink went flying, as dishes clattered to the ground and glasses shattered.

The room grew silent.

"All this food," Volstagg said, eyeing the remains of a large cake. "So innocent. Cast to the ground. It breaks the heart."

Thor shot him a look so cold that Volstagg took a step back as if he had been hit. Glancing around the room, Volstagg's gaze fell on Loki. He nodded at him as if to say, "Can you please do something about your wild brother?"

Loki doubted there was anything he could say or do. Still, he walked over, reaching out a hand to comfort Thor.

His brother stopped him. "It's unwise to be in my company right now," Thor said harshly.

"I think you're right," Loki said, not heeding his brother's advice. "The Jotuns deserve punishment for what they've done. But there's nothing we can do without defying Father."

As Loki spoke, Thor's pacing slowed, and a light gleamed in his eyes. Loki gulped. This was not good. Not good at all. It meant Thor had an idea, and while he may have been willing to risk the wrath of the king, Loki wasn't so eager to do so. He had spent too many years trying to get his father's attention, and he didn't want what attention he finally did get to come from a foolish idea of Thor's. His brother's next words confirmed his fears.

"We're going to Jotunheim," Thor stated.

"It's madness!" Loki cried, catching the attention of the others, who had been standing apart from the brothers.

"What sort of madness?" Volstagg asked.

"Nothing!" Loki answered, shooting his brother a look. "Thor was making a jest."

"The safety of our realm is no jest," Thor said, walking over to his fellow warriors and filling them in on his plan. "We're going to Jotunheim."

As Thor tried to convince the others, Loki moved to the side and absently listened. Why did he always seem to get into trouble because of his older brother? Wasn't he supposed to be the wiser one? Odin had expressly forbidden that they enter Jotunheim. Yet it wasn't the first time Thor had done something reckless. And it wouldn't be the first time Loki was powerless to stop him. Anger shot through him. Did Thor not realize what could happen if they were caught? Or worse, if they did go to Jotunheim and were overwhelmed by the Frost Giants? They would be realms away. Who would save them?

Sighing, he tuned back into the conversation to hear Thor say, "My friends, trust me now. We must do this." Then he turned to Loki and raised an eyebrow as if to say, "You are in, are you not, little brother?"

There was no choice. "I won't let my brother march into Jotunheim alone," he said simply.

❧❧

Early the next morning, Loki met his brother, the Warriors Three, and Lady Sif. The palace was quiet at that hour, with only a few attendants up and about, lighting fires in the hearths and working in the kitchen to prepare that day's meals.

Silently, they walked across the grounds to one of the stables where their horses waited, already saddled. Their armor had been gathered and now sat at the ready.

The night before, Loki had made a decision. True, he could not dictate his brother's actions, but that didn't mean he couldn't make plans of his own. As the others checked and double-checked that they had everything they would need for their journey to Jotunheim, Loki slipped away.

When Loki rejoined the others, they were just beginning to mount their horses. Hogun give him a curious glance, but he ignored it. What he had done was none of their business.

"We must first find a way to get past Heimdall," Thor was saying, referring to the huge warrior who guarded the Observatory and controlled the Bifrost and who would allow them access to Jotunheim.

"That will be no easy task," Volstagg

observed, trying to get his bulky body comfortable atop his horse. "It's said the gatekeeper can see a single dewdrop fall from a blade of grass a thousand miles away."

Loki tried not to roll his eyes. Heimdall was not nearly as powerful as Volstagg claimed. He couldn't be; or else how did the Jotuns manage to sneak past him? It would take a person with true power to make *that* happen. *That* was the type of person Volstagg should fear.

Fandral seemed to agree with Loki's thoughts. "And he can hear a cricket passing gas in Niffelheim," he said, his voice teasing.

"Forgive him!" Volstagg cried, raising his eyes to the sky. "He meaneth no offense!"

The others were still laughing at the big man's even bigger superstitions as they finally rode away from the palace. Within moments, they were through the tall gate that surrounded the royal city and riding across the Rainbow Bridge.

~⚬~

The Observatory sat at the edge of the realm. Behind it, the dark cosmos spread out, a black sea of twinkling lights, which made the domed building seem to float in the sky.

When they arrived, Heimdall was waiting for them.

"Leave this to me," Loki said, eyeing the intimidating man whose face was nearly hidden behind a gold helmet. "Good Heimdall—" Loki began to say.

The man held up a hand, silencing him. "You think you can deceive me?" he asked, and Loki took an involuntary step backward. How much did Heimdall know? He opened his mouth to protest, but the guard went on. "I, who can sense the flapping of a butterfly's wings across the cosmos?"

Volstagg eyed the others knowingly. Turning

to Loki, he teased, "Leaving it to you got us pretty far, didn't it?"

Loki glared at him. "Get me off this bridge before it cracks under your girth," he retorted.

Once again, Heimdall held up a hand to silence them. "You are not dressed warmly enough," he said, causing Loki to breathe a sigh of relief. So that was what Heimdall knew— that they were going to attack the icy realm of Jotunheim. Heimdall must have heard about the attack in the Vault and was anxious to figure out how the giants had slipped past them.

With a nod, the group followed Heimdall to the Observatory. Loki looked up and around at the large domed ceiling, its sides covered with carvings and glittering with an unnatural bronze light. As they all looked on, Heimdall walked over to what appeared to be a large control panel in the middle of the room. He lifted up his sword and plunged it deep into the device. The room suddenly filled with a pulsating, vibrating energy—the Bifrost. Turning, Loki saw a large opening on the side of the Observatory. Beyond it, the cosmos spread out.

Heimdall plunged his sword even deeper into the device, and the Bifrost energy quickened, coalescing into a vortex of spinning rainbow light. It shot out into the darkness, creating a link with Jotunheim.

"All is ready," Heimdall said. "You may pass."

Loki hated Bifrost travel. The way the portal sucked and pulled you apart until you feared you would not recover; the shock and cold as you were sucked between realms; and the knowledge that when the Bifrost closed behind you, it might not ever open again, trapping you far from home. Still, he had no choice. The plan was in motion, and this trip was part of it.

As Thor stepped up and disappeared into the vortex, Loki paused and looked back over his shoulder, as if he could see into the palace.

Turning back, he walked up to the portal entrance and took a deep breath.

One more step and he would be sucked into the swirling rainbow.

They were on their way to Jotunheim.

And what would happen once they got there was not in the hands of fate but in the hands of his impulsive brother and his warrior friends. . . .

THE POWER
OF THREE

Volstagg had never been this cold in his entire
life. Or hungry. It wasn't natural for one not to
feel one's nose or lips or hands or even eyeballs.
And it certainly wasn't natural for him to hear his
stomach grumbling over the sound of the wind
howling. No, it was entirely wrong. As was this
godforsaken journey to Jotunheim that he and his
fellow warriors had been talked into by Thor
Odinson.

Usually, Volstagg would be up for any adven-
ture. His giant size was only matched by his
equally large appetite for food—and excitement.
And he had been at Thor's side on many a journey. It was his rightful place as a member of the
Warriors Three. He, Fandral the Dashing (who, in

Volstagg's opinion, was a bit too attached to mir-
rors and his own reflection), and Hogun the Grim
(who was certainly grim, you couldn't argue with
that), were famous throughout the Nine Realms.
Poems had been written about the mighty band of
adventurers in Nornheim. Songs had been sung of
their trips to Midgard, and tales had been told of
their many conquests—of both lands outside the
realm and women. And they were all true—well,
most of them. At least the ones that other people
told. Volstagg himself believed that a bit of
embellishment could go a long way.

But unfortunately, he was not embellishing
now. It *was* cold. And he did *not* want to be in
Jotunheim.

Lifting his head slightly, Volstagg felt the
sting of ice against his cheeks. He did his best to
glare at Thor, who walked ahead of him, seem-
ingly unaffected by the temperature. Volstagg tried
to raise an eyebrow but his eyebrows were frozen,
so he fumed instead. They shouldn't be here. Odin

Allfather had expressly forbidden his son from traveling from Asgard to Jotunheim. But Thor did not take kindly to orders. And he certainly didn't take kindly to having his home invaded. Which the Jotuns had done—on the very day Thor was to become the new king of Asgard.

Jotunheim had slowly decayed until it was now nothing but a world of melting and cracking ice populated by angry and bitter Frost Giants. Still, their king was strong, and Asgard could not chance starting a war with them. That was why Odin had forbidden Thor from trying to take revenge, even if he didn't like it that his realm had been invaded. They couldn't risk a war.

Thor had raged, furious about being kept on a tight leash. If the day had gone according to plan, he would have been made king. And as king, *he* would have been the one making decisions.

Volstagg could have predicted what happened next: Thor had turned on the charm to get the Warriors Three to help him.

"My friends," he had said to the Warriors Three, Lady Sif, and Loki when the group had gathered in one of the great banquet halls, "have you forgotten all that we've done together?"

He turned to Hogun, undaunted by the man's grim expression and crossed arms. Thor was used to seeing the silent man with a scowl on his handsome face. While others quaked at the sight of the warrior whose large spiked mace was always by his side, Thor was never daunted—even on the occasions when he should be. Such as now. Still, he went on: "Who led you into the most glorious of battles?" he asked Hogun, who gave a measured nod in response.

Thor approached Fandrall, who was relishing his own reflection. "And who led you on adventures so dangerous that female admirers and adoring fans continue to follow you around to this day?"

Fandrall flashed his winning smile. "It was you, my prince." Fandrall said, proud of his exploits.

Then Thor walked over and put an arm around Volstagg. He had to reach up, as Volstagg was one of the few Asgardians taller than Thor. With his other hand he patted Volstagg's large belly. "And who led you to delicacies so succulent you thought you'd died and gone to Valhalla?"

"You did," Volstagg said, his stomach growling.

Thor smiled smugly. Finally he turned to Lady Sif. She was, as always, wearing a long sword across her back, and he knew all too well that there were more weapons hidden in her armor. While she was one of the most beautiful women in all the realms, her beauty was matched by her expert sword skills. No one dared mess with her. No one except Thor. "And who proved wrong all who scoffed at the idea that a young maiden could be one of the fiercest warriors this realm has ever known?" he asked.

She raised one perfectly arched eyebrow, and the corner of her mouth lifted up in the barest hint of a smile. "I did," she said simply.

The others let out a nervous laugh as Thor nodded. "True," he admitted. "But I supported you." Then he turned back to the rest of the group. "My friends, trust me now. We must do this."

And so they did.

∾≈∾

A piece of ice hit Volstagg in the cheek, bringing him abruptly back to the situation at hand. Once more, he cursed the Frost Giants for ever making this trip necessary.

Beside him, Fandral looked equally upset by the situation. The charming warrior hated to be anywhere he needed to cover his face. And he really did not like being far from women and a nice flagon of ale. Hogun walked a bit ahead. Volstagg couldn't tell how he was feeling, since the man looked as grim as he did on the sunniest of days on Asgard.

Thor was still irritatingly cheerful. "It feels

good, doesn't it?" he shouted over his shoulder. "To be together again, adventuring on another world."

"Is that what we're doing?" Fandral called back.

"What would you call it?" Thor asked, sounding honestly perplexed.

"Freezing," Fandral replied.

"Starving," Volstagg couldn't help but add.

Silence fell over the group as they continued to trek across the frozen wasteland. How could anything dangerous come from this realm? Volstagg wondered as he walked. It seemed completely abandoned. Occasionally they would pass what might have been a house or small village. But the buildings had long since fallen into disrepair, and only the faintest skeleton of a frame could sometimes be seen through the ice. Volstagg felt an involuntary shiver that had nothing to do with the cold. This realm had once been one of the mightiest and most feared of Asgard's enemies. But now, it seemed pitiful. Had Odin really caused such devastation? The Casket of Eternal Winters seemed a heavy price to pay, looking at the realm now. Perhaps the Frost Giants were right to want it back.

Volstagg shook off these thoughts. It was not his place to wonder. He was here to help Thor confront Laufey. And it looked as if that was about to happen. They had arrived at the central plaza of Jotunheim.

As soon as they walked into the plaza, the wind died down and the ice stopped pelting their faces. Cautiously, they took off the hoods that had been offering them a bit of protection and raised their eyes to scan their surroundings. Each warrior kept a steady hand near his weapons in case of ambush.

But they seemed to be alone. The only noise

came from the walls that creaked and melted around them and also from Volstagg's labored breathing. Fandral shot him a look. "Could you keep it down?" he said. "Or would you like them to know exactly where to throw their ice spears?"

"They would just need to see your shiny hair to know where to aim," Volstagg replied. "How much time did you spend brushing back those lovely locks of yours this morning? Ten minutes? An hour?"

"Hush," Lady Sif hissed. "Both of you. I don't think we're alone anymore."

And she was right. Volstagg felt the hairs on the back of his neck rise, as out of the shadows and from behind the crumbling columns, Frost Giants appeared. Their blue skin looked as cold as the rest of the planet, and they were very, *very* big. Even Volstagg looked small next to them. As they stepped into the light, he noticed that each giant had a different build. One of them had a large, wide, domed forehead while another had one arm that hung longer than the other and tapered into a very narrow hand.

"What is your business here?" one of the giants hissed.

Thor took a step forward, and in a choreographed move the giants took a step forward as well, tightening the circle around the Asgardians. "I speak only to your king," Thor said, his strong voice bouncing off the walls.

"Then speak," another voice replied from the shadows of a balcony above them.

Volstagg narrowed his eyes as he tried to make out the speaker. He caught a glimpse of a long, lean giant slowly making his way to the foreground. There was a slight stoop to his shoulders, which indicated that he might be old, but his voice was still full of pride. This must be the Frost Giant king.

As if in confirmation of Volstagg's thoughts, the giant stepped forward out of the shadows. "I am Laufey," he said, "king of this realm." His

THE MIGHTY THOR

SON OF ODIN ALLFATHER
HEIR TO THE THRONE OF ASGARD

The majestic and peaceful realm of Asgard.

Inside the palace, Thor raises his mighty hammer, Mjolnir, in
triumph as he greets his fellow citizens.

THE WARRIORS THREE

Together, they are Asgard's fiercest
combatants and Thor's closest friends.

FANDRAL THE DASHING   VOLSTAGG THE VOLUMINOUS   HOGUN THE GRIM

Queen Frigga confronts King Odin about his decision to banish their son Thor to Earth.

Heimdall, the all-seeing guardian, watches over the Bifrost which allows Asgardians to travel between realms.

LOKI
MASTER OF MAGIC

Laufey, king of the **Frost Giants** and **ruler** of the icy realm of Jotunheim, sits on his throne and plans his revenge against Asgard.

After being insulted by the Frost Giants, Thor's dangerous and impulsive actions on Jotunheim led him to banishment on Midgard.

JANE FOSTER

ASTROPHYSICIST

A massive funnel cloud brings a metal monster to New Mexico and it threatens to annihilate the town, and Thor.

A powerless Thor prepares to battle with Asgard's most fearsome and dangerous weapon—the Destroyer.

voice crackled as he spoke, like the ice that melted and broke apart all around him.

Volstagg had heard many tales of the famed king of the Frost Giants, mostly from Thor and Loki who had heard Odin's stories growing up. He knew the king had no fear of battle. His fierce fighting style was only second to Odin's, and over the years he'd lost many Jotuns to battles between the various realms. Seeing the king now, Volstagg could believe the stories. Despite the state of his realm, Laufey looked noble and far too proud to reveal the giants had suffered at all.

"I demand answers!" Thor called up to the king, obviously unconcerned with the giant's reputation. "How did your people get into Asgard?"

"The house of Odin is full of traitors," Laufey said cryptically.

Turning, Volstagg exchanged a confused glance with Fandral and Hogun. Traitors? What was Laufey talking about? Asgard had no traitors.

Thor apparently agreed. His grip on his hammer tightened and he took another step forward. "Do not dishonor my father's name with your lies!" he cried.

"Why have you come here?" Laufey asked rhetorically. "To make peace? No. You long for battle." From the look on the king's face, Volstagg guessed that the giant would be happy to oblige.

As if on cue, a few more Frost Giants stepped into view. This was not good.

Lady Sif seemed to feel the same way. She shot Loki a look, hoping Thor's younger brother would take the hint. He needed to say something—now.

Loki, who had been rather silent up until this point, nodded. Walking over, he put a warning hand on his brother's arm. "Stop and think," he said, trying to reason with his hotheaded brother. "We are outnumbered."

Thor dragged his gaze, which had been fixed

on Laufey, away from the balcony. Shaking off his brother's arm, he looked around. For the first time, he seemed to notice the Frost Giants. Perhaps his brother was right. Perhaps it would be wiser to leave now. Still . . . he had come here for a fight. Looking over, he eyed the Warriors Three and Lady Sif. They were all shaking their heads, and he could easily read their looks—they wanted to leave, too.

With one last glance at Laufey, Thor sighed and turned to go. Behind him, he heard Volstagg say, "Thank Yggdrasil." Then Fandral laughed softly. Perhaps this is what his father had meant about being wise and patient, Thor thought. True, they had not taken revenge, but neither had they caused irreconcilable damage.

And then one of the Frost Giants spoke.

"Run back home, little princess," it said.

A few more minutes, Volstagg thought. Why couldn't that giant have waited just a few more minutes to say something?

Volstagg saw Thor lift his mighty hammer. Slowly, and with a heavy sigh, Volstagg drew his axe, Hogun clutched his mace, and Lady Sif pulled out her double-bladed sword. Reluctantly, Fandral reached for his sword and held it in front of him. Volstagg had to stifle a laugh as he caught his friend checking out his reflection in the blade's smooth metal. The Asgardians then formed a circle around Thor. Above all else, they would protect the prince.

It seemed the Jotuns were intent on protecting their own as well. They reached down and touched the puddles of chilled water at their feet. Instantly, the water traveled up their limbs and onto their bodies, freezing into weapons of various kinds. Volstagg saw the giant he had noticed earlier with the narrow hand. The ice froze over his lean limb, creating a sharp spear. The giant with the round head now had a mallet which he could ram into objects—or Asgard warriors. Another stepped in front of Fandral and created a sword and spiked armor out of the water. The ice glinted and sparkled dangerously.

"I'm hoping that's just decorative," Fandral said.

But it wasn't. The battle was on.

The sound of clashing metal and ice filled the plaza as Frost Giants and Asgardians faced off. Volstagg sighed as the mallet-headed giant raced at him. Stepping to the side at the last moment, the giant ran right by him and crashed into a wall. The palace shook with the blow. "Maybe next time," Volstagg said merrily before turning to another approaching giant. Beside him, Fandral ducked and weaved, his sword swishing through the air as he confidently dispatched giant after giant. Despite the overwhelming odds, he seemed to be having a good time.

Even Hogun looked pleased. Or, rather, at least a little less grim. Out of the corner of his eye, Volstagg watched Hogun face off against one of the giants. Hogun was clearly winning when the giant suddenly managed to back him up against one of the walls. He pulled his sword arm back, ready to strike. Hogun raised his mace high over his head, embedding it in the wall above. As the giant plunged forward, Hogun swung up and over him. Then, in midair, he pulled the mace out of the wall and landed behind the giant. With one swift move, he knocked the Jotun, now unconscious, aside.

But the Jotuns kept coming. Volstagg knew the giants needed to be stopped soon. The longer the battle continued, the worse the odds. The treacherous Frost Giants outnumbered them. To overtake them, the Asgardians would have to do something bold, something daring, something only the Warriors Three were capable of.

Fandral seemed to be on the same page as Volstagg as he yelled out, "What move do you think?"

Volstagg stepped out of the way of an

approaching Jotun and then used his giant belly to knock him over. "I say we use the Norn's Revenge," he shouted back.

"At this close range?" Fandral replied, swiping the frozen arm off of one of the giants. "I think the Alfheim Lunge is a better move."

Volstagg paused. The Alfheim Lunge. It *could* work . . . perhaps. But it was rather embarrassing. And they had only done it that one time. Just as his mind started to drift back to that day, a blast of cold air startled Volstagg into the present.

The Alfheim Lunge, as the Warriors Three had dubbed it upon their arrival back in Asgard, was indeed a useful trick. But they were in the middle of a heated battle. It did not seem the time. He was just about to ask Fandral for another idea when Hogun rushed past him.

"Shut up!" he ordered. "And fight!"

Volstagg took an involuntary step back and had to duck as a Frost Giant swung a large block of ice at him. Hogun never spoke in battle. It was one of his rules. So if he was breaking it now, they were in far more danger than Volstagg had thought. Swinging around with his sword in hand, Volstagg sent the giant flying into a deep crevasse. Then he turned and held his weapon at the ready.

Across the way, Fandral continued to dodge and weave as he took out more Jotuns. Right outside the plaza, Lady Sif was holding her own, her shield raised and her sword swishing back and forth so fast it was almost impossible to see. Glancing behind him, Volstagg saw that Thor was busy defending himself as well. A circle of giants had formed around him as though he were in an arena and they were each waiting their turn to fight him. His hammer swung wildly, crackling with light and energy.

So far, the tide was on their side. But that could change any minute. The giants kept coming, and the Asgardians had no backup. It was going to be a difficult fight.

Turning back to the Jotuns in front of him, Volstagg let out a mighty roar and charged into the fray. No, now was not the time for the Alfheim Lunge. That was a move to use another time, in another battle.

Today, they just had to survive, and they would only do so thanks to Odin Allfather. He would intervene on their behalf, but the cost of their foolishness would be high. Thor would be banished from Asgard, but the Warriors Three would live to fight again another day. And that day would come sooner than any of them expected. Their battlefield would be the realm of Midgard, the precise location of Thor's exile. But we're getting ahead of ourselves. . . .

A STRANGER'S
ARRIVAL

The desert air was dry and still. In the small town of Puente Antiguo, New Mexico, the stores were closed for the night, and the houses were quiet. The local residents were tucked inside, eating dinner or watching television. Parked on the only street that led in and out of town was an old, beat-up Pinzgauer utility vehicle. A young woman sat in the driver's seat, staring out at the desert just beyond, while next to her, an older gentleman read through various papers on his lap.

The van started up and headed out of town into the dark desert. For a while, there was only the sound of the wind through the open windows and the occasional beep from the computers.

Finally, about twenty miles outside town, the van came to a stop. They had arrived at their destination.

In the back of the Pinzgauer, Jane Foster sat in front of a row of computer monitors and a variety of other scientific equipment. Most everything in the Pinzgauer—including the utility vehicle itself—had seen better days. The monitors were held together by duct tape, and some of the equipment was generations behind the most recent models, though Jane did manage to sneak in some very high-tech machines. As an astrophysicist who studied the stars for signs of spatial anomalies, she didn't have a lot of people pounding down the door to give her funding for research or equipment.

But that would change soon enough. She was sure of it. Her work in New Mexico was getting her closer and closer to actual findings. And if tonight's readings were any indication, something big was about to happen. Something *very* big. Popping her head over the front seat, she looked at the young woman who was driving. Darcy Lewis had just joined the team as a college intern but so far, she seemed less interested in science than in surfing the Internet. Still, she was a good driver. "Thanks for the ride, Darcy," Jane said now.

Turning to the older gentleman, she smiled. "Hold on to your seat, Selvig."

Erik Selvig smiled but didn't say anything. Dr. Selvig was a colleague and friend of Jane's father, and he knew that her potential was limitless. He just wished she had chosen a field of study that was more easily accepted by the rest of the scientific community. While he had always believed in her, he feared her ideas might be too far ahead of their time for the rest of the world. Selving's thoughts were interrupted by the beeping from one of Jane's computers.

The beeping increased, and Jane opened the large sunroof. Stepping up on the bench built into the vehicle's side, she raised herself up and into the night. In her hand she held a magnetometer. With it, she could calibrate the position of the stars. A digital display read 00:00:19, and it was counting down.

"Here we go . . ." she said, excitement in her voice as she stared up at the sky. Selvig joined her. "In three . . . two . . . one . . . now!"

Nothing happened.

"Wait for it," Jane said.

Still nothing.

Leaning out the front window, Darcy looked up at Jane. "Can I turn on the radio?" she asked. It was pretty boring out there in the dark.

Jane shot her a look. "No," she snapped.

Frustrated, Jane sank back into the van. Selvig's expression was sympathetic. He knew how much this night had meant to Jane. He watched as she opened a notebook full of notes and calculations. She didn't go anywhere without that notebook. It held her life's work. Which, at the moment, seemed useless. If she couldn't prove to Selvig—who believed in her—that she had actual data that added up to something, she would never be able to convince a stranger. This was her last chance.

"The last seventeen occurrences have been predictable to the *second*, Erik!" she cried. She ran a hand through her light brown hair, her usually beautiful features marred by tension. "I just don't understand."

Turning back to her monitors, she began to rerun the calculations, looking for an error in her numbers, something, *anything*, to explain why nothing had happened. Focused on the screens, she didn't notice the odd glowing clouds that had formed in the sky. They came out of nowhere, their edges tinted in faint rainbow colors.

Darcy, however, did notice. "Jane?" she said over her shoulder.

"What!?" Jane shouted back. Now was not

the time to ask about music or if Darcy could do her nails or whatever it was that her assistant wanted.

But then Darcy said, "I think you want to see this." Her tone was serious, so Jane lifted her head and looked through the front window.

Her jaw dropped.

In front of her was something unlike anything she had ever seen before. It looked as if the constellations had been sucked down from the sky and had gathered in a huge cloud. The rainbow light had grown stronger, brightening the area of the desert above which the cloud hovered.

"Drive!" she shouted to Darcy before turning around and grabbing a camera.

As the Pinzgauer raced through the night, Jane popped up out of the sunroof again and began filming. Her mind raced with the possibilities of what this could mean. Funding would be no problem once people got ahold of this footage. It was unbelievable. Then she frowned. Was it too unbelievable?

"You're seeing it too, right?" she asked Selvig.

Popping his head up through the roof, he nodded, and Jane relaxed. That was good news.

The winds grew stronger. At the center of the clouds, a dark mass began to swirl faster and faster, forming a tornado. The strange rainbow light grew even brighter. "We've got to get closer!" Jane shouted to Darcy just as a huge bolt of lightning cut through the clouds and struck the ground. The Pinzgauer rocked on its wheels, and Darcy struggled to keep the vehicle level.

"That's it!" she cried. "I'm done! I'm not dying for six college credits!" Yanking the wheel with both hands, she tried to turn the van. But Jane wasn't about to let that happen. Jumping forward, she reached toward the wheel and tried to grab it. The two struggled for control while the wind outside whipped and howled. The van's headlights bounced over the desert, illuminating the form of a large man!

The man stumbled out of the storm, his clothes tattered and his eyes dazed. Looking up, Jane only had a moment to see confusion in his striking blue eyes. Jerking the wheel, she tried to avoid him but—BAM! The van sideswiped the man, sending him flying.

The car came to a stop, and a shocked silence filled the space as Jane, Darcy, and Selvig stared first at each other and then at the crumpled body of the man on the ground. Then, as if jolted by electricity, they all leaped out of the car, Jane in the lead. She raced over to the man's side and kneeled down, hoping and praying that she would find him breathing.

But she hadn't expected or hoped to find the handsomest man she had ever seen. His features looked as though they had been sculpted out of marble by a master, and his chest was wide and his shoulders chiseled. His long blond hair lay undisturbed despite the windy conditions, and Jane had the overwhelming urge to run her hands through it. *I hit a model*, Jane thought as she stared at him. *This is going to get me in so much trouble.*

"Do me a favor," she said, "and don't be dead, okay?"

At the sound of her voice, the man groaned, and his eyelids fluttered. Then eyes of the deepest azure locked on Jane, and for a moment she forgot to breathe.

Shaking her head, Jane rocked back on her heels. She needed to get a grip. She was more levelheaded than this. Clearly, this evening's events had made her a bit more emotional than she usually was, and the stress of hitting this guy was making her feel sympathy for him, nothing more. She was a scientist. Not some foolish young girl falling head over heels in love with a stranger. Yes, she thought again, it's just the night making me think foolish things.

Then, as if to prove her point, the storm clouds suddenly vanished and the wind calmed. If she hadn't been right in the middle of it, Jane would never have known the night had turned so stormy. And why, she wondered, did it seem connected with this man lying in front of her?

Looking back down at him, she narrowed her gaze. Where had he come from?

A few uneasy moments passed. Then the man lying on the ground in front of Jane sat up abruptly, startling her. Staggering to his feet, he gazed down at his clothes, then up at the sky, and then back at Jane, who still sat on the desert floor. Stumbling from the impact, the stranger looked at them with a mixture of disappointment and disgust.

"Are you okay?" Jane asked, realizing even

as she spoke that it was a rather silly question since he was obviously fine, though a bit disoriented.

The blond man didn't answer. Instead, he continued to scan the ground. "Hammer," he finally said.

Jane didn't know what to say to that. She was about to respond when out of the corner of her eye, she saw odd markings etched in the sand near where the man had landed. "We've got to move fast, before anything changes," she said, her earlier excitement returning. Jane grabbed handfuls of soil samples, hoping to run a battery of tests on the earth when they got back to the lab. Then she realized it would be good to write everything down, so she reached for her notebook.

In fact, Jane was so absorbed in her work that she didn't notice Selvig and Darcy giving her odd looks. Finally, Selvig spoke. "Jane," he said gently, "we need to get him to a hospital." He nodded in the direction of the large man who was wandering around the area, looking lost and sad despite his imposing size.

Jane shook her head and kneeled down to scoop up another soil sample. "Look at him," she said absently, "he's fine."

"FATHER! HEIMDALL!" the man screamed, raising his hands to the sky. "Open the bridge!"

So maybe he wasn't completely fine. But Jane wasn't about to waste time taking a mental case to the hospital when there was so much to go over here. "You and Darcy take him to the hospital," she said. "I'll stay here."

As she spoke, the man approached Darcy. "You!" he said, his voice booming in the quiet desert. "What world is this? Alfheim? Nornheim?"

"Uh . . . New Mexico," Darcy said, raising an eyebrow. What was this guy on? He may have been the hottest thing she'd ever seen, but he was seriously loopy.

Suddenly, he whirled, his expression furious.

Darcy took an involuntary step back and reached into her pocket for the taser she always carried with her. Holding it up in front of her, she tried to keep her finger from shaking.

"You dare threaten Thor with so puny a—"

Thor, as he called himself, didn't get to finish. Darcy fired and he fell to the ground, convulsing with the electrical jolts from the taser. A moment later, he was unconscious.

Looking at the man on the ground and then at Darcy, Jane sighed. It seemed she would be going to the hospital after all.

Puente Antiguo was not a busy town, even in the middle of the day. But in the dead of night, it was practically a ghost town. The county hospital was no different. A few townies roamed the emergency room, having been dropped off after spending a bit too much time at the local tavern. The skeleton crew of nurses and doctors barely gave them any notice. Apparently, this happened almost every night.

What did *not* happen every night was having a man like Thor brought into the place. With considerable effort, Jane, Selvig, and Darcy managed to get him from the van onto a gurney. Leaving the others to keep an eye on him, Jane made her way to the admitting area. A young nurse sat behind the desk, filing her nails. Jane cleared her throat.

Looking up, the nurse smiled. Then, in a manner that could only be described as painstaking, she began the process of admitting Thor.

"Name?" she asked, her fingers poised over the keyboard.

"He said it was Thor," Jane answered.

The nurse typed out each letter with one finger. T-H-O-R. "And your relationship to him?"

"I've never met him before," Jane said.

"Until she hit him with the car," Darcy added helpfully.

Jane shot her a look. "*Grazed* him, actually. And *she* tasered him," she quickly added, trying to make the tasering sound worse than hitting him with her car.

"I'm going to need a name and contact number," the nurse said, either too tired or not bright enough to care that Jane had just admitted to hitting a man with her car. As Jane spelled out her name, the nurse once again slowly typed each letter. Click-click-click. Jane felt her shoulders tensing and she was just about to scream when Selvig walked over and handed his card to the nurse.

"You can reach us there," he said simply. Then turning, he walked out of the emergency room, Jane and Darcy following.

They had done what they could for "Thor." There was nothing left to do. It was now in the hands of the hospital.

Then why, Jane thought as they walked away, do I feel like I shouldn't leave him?

Sighing, she shrugged off the thought. She had tons of data to go through and soil samples to test. She had her hands full enough without the addition of a strange, albeit handsome, man. It was time to go back to her office and get to work.

❧❧

When Jane had arrived in Puente Antiguo, there had been little in the way of free office space for rent. So she had settled on what there had been—an abandoned car dealership that had been empty for years. The old sign that read SMITH MOTORS still rose from the roof, a reminder of better days when the town had been more prosperous. Early the next morning, Jane sat hunched over a workstation. The sun rose over the distant mountains through the large windows behind her, making them gleam and sparkle. Jane didn't notice. She was busy soldering a piece of equipment while a printer churned out images she had taken of the previous night's storm. Selvig walked into the lab holding two cups of coffee. He placed one in front of Jane and then took a sip from his.

"We might want to perform a spectral analysis," he suggested softly.

Jane looked up, surprised. "We?" she repeated. She wanted to squeal with excitement but kept her composure.

"These anomalies might signify something bigger," she said, indicating an image on the monitor. It showed the giant cloud they had seen the night before. As the image shifted, the cloud disappeared, and a blisterlike object appeared in its place. It bulged outward like a balloon, and it appeared to be covered in stars. Jane waited for Selvig to absorb what he was seeing and then she spoke again. "I think the lensing around the edges is characteristic of an Einstein-Rosen Bridge."

Darcy, who had been doodling in her note-book while she waited for each of the pictures to print, looked up, confused.

"A wormhole," Jane explained in layman's terms. What she didn't say was that it appeared the wormhole, if it was one, had opened into a place unknown to any scientist or astrophysicist. The constellation of stars they saw was brand new.

A moment later, Darcy's voice broke into Jane's thoughts. "Hey, check it out," she said.

Jane turned, about to chastise Darcy for inter-rupting her, but the words died on her lips. Darcy was holding up a picture of the funnel cloud of stars. And there, in the middle of it, as if being shot down from the heavens like a bolt of light-ning, was the unmistakable image of a man. Thor.

All three were silent as they tried to process what this meant.

"I think I left something at the hospital," Jane finally said.

Racing toward the door, she hoped that Thor would still be there.

❦

Yet when they arrived, Room 102 was empty. The bed was overturned, and the IV stand lay on the ground. Clearly, Thor had decided to check himself out. Sighing, Jane went back to the parking lot.

"So, now what?" Darcy said when she saw that Jane was alone.

"We find him," Jane answered. "Our data won't tell us what it was like inside the event. He can."

This Thor person, whoever he was, was the most important piece of information Jane had. There was no way she was going to just let him disappear. Of course it had nothing whatsoever to do with the fact that he was incredibly handsome and had made her heart race wildly. No, it had nothing to do with that. It was all about the science.

Getting in the driver's seat, she put the car in reverse, stepped on the gas, and—WHAM! She hit something—again. With a groan, she looked in the rearview mirror. She had hit Thor—again! Dressed in hospital scrubs, he lay on the ground in a position eerily similar to the one from the night before.

Leaping out of the car, she raced around to the back and kneeled down. "I'm so sorry!" she cried. "I *swear* I'm not doing that on purpose."

Thor didn't say anything for a moment. He simply gazed up at the sun, which was now high in the sky, its rays warming the pavement. "Blue sky, one sun," he said softy. Then he groaned. "Oh, no. This is Earth, isn't it?"

Back at her trailer behind the lab, Jane rummaged through her drawers, hoping to find something that might come close to fitting Thor. She grabbed an old pair of jeans and a T-shirt and brought them into the lab and handed them to Thor. Nodding over her shoulder, she told him he could change in the back. Then she went to join Darcy.

A moment later, he walked back into the main part of the lab bare-chested and holding the shirt in one hand. Jane's mouth went dry.

"You know, for a crazy homeless guy, he's pretty cut," Darcy observed, glancing between Thor and Jane in amusement. She had only worked for Jane for a little while, but she had never seen her boss act like this. It made her seem less like a superscientist and more like a human being.

Walking over, Thor held up the shirt. A sticker on the front of it was peeling off. It read: "Hello, my name is Dr. Donald Blake."

Jane blushed and quickly ripped the sticker off. "My ex," she explained. "They're the only clothes I had that'll fit you."

Thor took the shirt back and put it on over his head. When he was fully dressed, he began to walk around the lab, glancing at the various schematics and drawings that covered the drawing boards and walls. He stopped in front of the collection of pictures from the storm Darcy had posted.

"What were you doing in that?" Jane asked, walking over and pointing to the picture in the center. Thor's outline could clearly be seen floating in the middle of the cloud.

Thor looked closer and then shrugged. "What does anyone do in the Bifrost?" he said dismissively.

Bifrost? Jane wrote the word in her notebook.

Why did that sound familiar? And why did Thor act as though this was nothing special? Who *was* he? She felt a tug in her gut, as though the answer were staring her in the face. But she shrugged it off. She probably just needed some sleep.

Thor, on the other hand, needed food. "This mortal form has grown weak," he said.

Clearly, Jane wasn't going to get answers right away. It would be best to give Thor what he wanted and then start again. "I can help with that," she said. Turning to Selvig and Darcy she added, "Let's go to Isabella's."

A short while later, the four sat in a booth at the only diner in town. Thor hadn't been kidding. He really was hungry. There was enough food on the table in front of him to feed all of them. There was a platter of steak and eggs, a tall stack of pancakes, and a dozen biscuits covered with gravy. Thor scooped up a mouthful of eggs and drowned it with a large swig of coffee. "This drink," he said, "I like it." Then he threw the mug down to the floor, shattering it and causing the other patrons to jump in their seats. "Another!"

Jane looked over at the diner's owner and smiled apologetically. "Sorry, Izzy," she said. Then, turning back to Thor, she hissed, "What was that?"

"It was delicious," Thor said. "I want another."

He sounded like a petulant little boy. "Then you should just say so," she instructed, embarrassed by Thor's thoughtless behavior.

"I just did," Thor replied, looking confused.

"I meant just ask for it," she said.

As Thor took another bite of his pancakes, two of the local residents entered the diner and took a seat at the counter. Jane had seen them around. Jake and Pete. They were known in Puente Antiguo for spending a bit too much time in the bar. However, at the moment they looked sober. Smiling at Isabella, they ordered cups of coffee.

"You missed all the excitement out at the crater," Jake said loud enough for Jane to hear.

Pete nodded excitedly. "They're saying some kind of satellite crashed."

At the mention of "satellite," Selvig perked up. "What did it look like?" he asked, getting up and walking over.

"Don't know nothing about the satellite," Jake answered, "but it was heavy! Nobody could lift it."

At that, Thor leaped to his feet, rattling the dishes and causing Jane to almost choke on her coffee. His eyes were wild as he rushed over and put his face right in Jake's. "Where?" he demanded.

Jake gulped visibly and tried to back away from the strange man in front of him. "Uh-uh-about fifty miles west of here," he said, his voice shaking.

Turning, Thor walked out of the restaurant.

"Where are you going?" Jane asked, rushing after him. This guy was acting stranger and stranger. But she couldn't risk letting him leave again. He still hadn't helped her.

"To get what belongs to me," Thor said. Then he stopped, as though it had just occurred to him that he had no idea where he was going. He looked at Jane. "If you take me there now, I'll tell you everything you wish to know."

Jane raised an eyebrow. "Everything?"

"All the answers you seek will be yours— once I reclaim Mjolnir."

Mjolnir? Jane repeated silently. What was Mjolnir and why did it sound like something Selvig would mutter when he was angry?

As if he could read her mind, Selvig pulled Jane aside. "Listen to what he's saying," Selvig insisted. " 'Thor.' 'Bifrost.' 'Mjolnir.' These are the stories I grew up with as a child . . . in Scandinavia!"

Jane looked back and forth between the two men. True, Thor could maybe answer her questions, but Selvig had never let her down. Maybe he was right, maybe this was a fool's errand.

"I'm sorry," she finally said. "I can't take you."

"I understand," Thor said. "Then this is where we say good-bye." Taking her hand, he raised it gently to his lips and after bowing to the others, walked off.

Jane watched him go, and for the first time in a long time, she wondered if her head was not as smart as her heart.

FINDING ANSWERS

Jane Foster's life had been turned upside down overnight. First, she had discovered a man in the middle of the desert. A man who, according to pictures she had taken herself, had fallen to Earth out of a rainbow-colored tornado. Then, this same man had made cryptic references to answering all her questions only to kiss her hand and disappear into the desert in search of a fallen "satellite."

Yet none of that had prepared her to walk back into her lab at Smith Motors and find it being raided by what appeared to be government agents. In the parking lot, men ripped equipment out of the Pinzgauer, transferring it into large black vans. More agents came out of the lab, holding boxes and files in their arms.

Jane rushed forward and burst into the lab, her heart pounding and her fists clenched. "What is going on here?!" she demanded.

One of the men stepped toward her. He was slight, with thinning brown hair and a warm, friendly face. He held out a hand. "Ms. Foster," he said, "I'm Agent Coulson, with S.H.I.E.L.D. We're investigating a security threat."

S.H.I.E.L.D.? What the heck was S.H.I.E.L.D.? Was it some part of the FBI or CIA that they kept hidden, like in those crazy cop shows? Jane had the uncomfortable feeling that this had something to do with Thor's arrival. It was too big a coincidence.

"We need to appropriate your equipment," Coulson went on, "and all your atmospheric data."

"By appropriate, you mean steal?" Jane snapped. As if it weren't obvious that they were taking whatever they wanted, permission or no. "We're on the verge of understanding something extraordinary." She held up her notebook as proof.

Coulson leaned down and picked up the box at his feet. Then, reaching out, he snatched the notebook out of Jane's hand and placed it on top of the pile. "Thank you for your cooperation," he said, and turning, left the lab. A moment later, the rest of the agents left as well.

Silence fell over the room as Jane, Selvig, and Darcy took in the damage. There was nothing left but a few small pieces of paper stuck beneath thumbtacks and a couple of loose pages of printer paper lying on the floor.

"Years of research, gone," Jane said, defeated. "They took our backups! They took the *backups* to our backups."

Selvig reached out a hand to comfort her, but she shook it off. He couldn't help her. No one could. Then she looked out the window and a sliver of hope blossomed. Across the street she saw Thor. He hadn't made it to the crater yet after all.

Smiling, she raced outside. She had an idea.

Thor was going to help her get her research back.

✦✦✦

A few minutes later, she and Thor were in the Pinzgauer heading twelve miles east of Puente Antiguo. The sun was beginning to set, and storm clouds were forming in the evening sky. Jane concentrated on the rough terrain, but out of the corner of her eye she snuck glances at Thor. He looked excited, almost as though he were going into battle. Jane, on the other hand, wasn't as confident.

"I've never done anything like this before," she said, breaking the silence.

"You're brave to do it," Thor replied, glancing over at her. For the first time since she'd hit him, he gave her a genuine smile.

"They just stole my entire life's work. I really don't have anything left to lose," Jane said.

"You're clever," Thor said. "Far more clever than anyone else in this realm." She shot him a confused look. "You think me strange?" he asked.

Jane caught the laugh that threatened to bubble out of her. Strange? That was putting it mildly. "Who are you?" she asked, trying to change the subject, or at least to start getting answers.

Thor nodded. "You'll see soon enough," he said, looking up ahead.

Jane followed his gaze, and her eyes grew wide. They had found the satellite. Parking the Pinzgauer, Jane and Thor made their way to the edge of the valley ridge and lay down on their stomachs. Pulling out a pair of binoculars, Jane looked down. The valley was illuminated with bright lights that reached high into the night and spanned outward. Guard towers were set up with armed men sitting inside, while other men and women rushed about on the ground. A glass-walled command trailer was at the center of the station, and Jane could just make out something beyond it. It looked small and dark and was partially buried in the ground. The satellite! There were massive tubes and wires that snaked around the grounds, leading in and out of what appeared to be temporary offices. On the side of one of the buildings, Jane saw the word S.H.I.E.L.D. written in bold white letters.

She turned and looked over at Thor. It seemed what she was looking for and what he was looking for were in the same place.

Getting to his feet, Thor shrugged off his jacket and handed it to Jane. "You're going to need this," he said.

"Why?" Jane asked. As if in response, thunder rolled across the desert sky. Jane could have sworn Thor had *told* the thunder to do that.

"Stay here," he said, ignoring her question. "Once I have Mjolnir, I will return what they stole from you." He looked her deep in the eyes. "Deal?"

"No!" Jane hissed, surprising both her and Thor. "Look what's down there! You can't just walk in, grab our stuff, and walk out!"

"No," Thor agreed and Jane felt her shoulders relax. And then he added, "I'm going to fly out."

Turning, he walked away, leaving Jane lying there with her mouth open. As he slipped into the valley, the first drops of rain began to fall.

A short while later, the Pinzgauer screeched into the parking lot at Smith Motors. Jane leaped out and raced inside. "I can't just leave him there!" she cried when she saw Selvig and Darcy. The two had been attempting to clean up the mess left by the S.H.I.E.L.D. agents. Darcy, however, had been distracted by a children's picture book that had somehow been left behind.

Flipping through it, she half-listened as Jane

filled Selvig in on what had happened out in the desert. Suddenly, a word on one of the pages caught her eye. "Hey! Look!" she shouted. The word looked an awful lot like the one Thor kept repeating. And above the word was an image of a hammer.

Jane walked over and grabbed the book from Darcy. "Where did you find this?"

Selvig answered: "In the children's section. I wanted to show you how ridiculous Thor's story is."

"Aren't you the one who's always told me to chase down all possibilities?" Jane said. "If that's really an Einstein-Rosen Bridge out there, then there's something on the other side. Advanced beings could have come through it before." Like Thor and his hammer, she added silently.

For a moment, no one said anything. Jane had never dared challenge her mentor before, but there were just too many signs pointing to the fact that Thor, whoever he was, was *not* from

Earth. And now he was trapped by agents intent on covering up his existence.

Finally, Selvig spoke. "I don't know what any of this means, Jane," he said. "But I'll help you because it's *you*." Sevlig didn't want Thor staying in Puente Antiguo. It was too dangerous . . . for all of them. But he also knew that Jane needed information from Thor. And despite his reservations, he knew that Jane would eventually guilt him into helping her.

Selvig grimaced at Jane, who let out a breath that she hadn't realized she was holding.

"Thank you, Selvig," she said.

He nodded and went to make a call. Now all she could do was wait and hope whatever plan Selvig came up with would work.

❧❧

The next few hours passed slowly. Every time the wind blew or a car passed by the lab, Jane jumped. Finally, Darcy sent her to the trailer to get some rest, insisting that she'd tell her when Selvig and Thor returned.

Just as Jane was falling into a fitful sleep, there was a loud rapping on the door. Jumping up, she threw it open to see Thor standing there, Selvig thrown over one shoulder. Jane's hand went to her heart, and she let out a loud gasp. "What happened?" she said. "Is he . . . ?" She didn't dare say the word aloud. But then Selvig groaned and mumbled something about gods of thunder and realms, and she caught the unmistakable odor of the tavern.

It seemed Selvig and Thor had gone out to celebrate Thor's escape from S.H.I.E.L.D. She should have known.

Gesturing behind her, Jane stepped aside so Thor could come in. There was something different about him. He seemed quieter, less sure of himself. She wondered what had happened after she'd left the base to make him act this way.

Gently, Thor placed Selvig on the bed and then patted the old man's cheek. Yes, Jane thought, something must have happened.

Then she realized Thor was no longer looking at Selvig but glancing around the trailer at the empty pizza boxes, old newspapers, and cookie wrappers. "Can we go outside?" Jane suggested.

Thor nodded, and they walked out of the trailer and headed over to the lab. On the roof, Jane had set up some chairs and a telescope and there were a few blankets.

"I come up here sometimes when I can't sleep," she explained. "Or when I'm trying to reconcile particle data. Or when Darcy's driving me crazy." She paused as a smile crept over Thor's face. "I come up here a lot, now that I think about it."

Thor didn't say anything. Instead, he just looked up at the night sky, as if it could provide him with answers. Once again Jane was struck with the clear sense that the Thor she had known this morning was different from this Thor. This Thor seemed more human despite the impressive muscles.

Finally, he spoke up, his deep and somber voice in the stillness of the night startling Jane. "You've been very kind," he said. "I've been far less grateful than you deserve."

"I also hit you with my car a couple times, so it kind of evens out," Jane said, teasing him.

Thor grinned and nodded. Then he reached into the pocket of his pants and pulled out Jane's notebook. He held it out to her. "It was all I could get back," he said apologetically. "Not as much as I promised. I'm sorry."

Jane took the notebook and opened it gently, as though scared it would disappear again. He had no idea how important this notebook was. It meant that she wouldn't have to start from scratch. That she could still prove her hypothesis. It was the greatest thing he could have gotten back. "Thank you," she said softly.

Then her face clouded over.

"What's wrong?" Thor asked, concerned.

"S.H.I.E.L.D.," she answered. "Whatever they are, they're never going to let this research see the light of day."

"You must finish what you've started."

"Why?" Jane asked, surprised at the urgency in his tone. And the confidence.

"Because you're right," he said simply. "It's taken so many generations for your people to get to this point. You're nearly there. You just need someone to show you how close you really are."

As he spoke, Thor moved closer. Jane's heart hammered in her chest as he reached over and took her notebook from her hands. Opening it to the image of what he called the Bifrost, he smiled. He was going to show her just how close she really was.

The next morning, Jane woke and stretched. Then she opened her eyes and smiled. Thor slept next to her, the rising sun turning his blond hair golden. They had stayed up all night talking about the Rainbow Bridge, the Bifrost, and the Nine Realms of Yggdrasil, including Asgard, where Thor was from, and Earth, or Midgard. Her mind was spinning with information, yet she also felt oddly at peace. She and Thor had shared something special last night. He had opened her eyes to so many things, and she had opened her life up to him. She wondered what that would mean for their future.

Beside her, Thor let out a small sigh and then his eyes fluttered open. Looking over at her, he smiled. "Breakfast?" he suggested.

A half-hour later, the smell of bacon and pancakes filled the lab. Jane sat at a table with Selvig and Darcy, trying to explain everything Thor had taught her. At the kitchen sink, Thor happily attempted to do the dishes. Jane looked over at him, quietly impressed.

"They're fascinating theories, Jane," Selvig said, looking at the new notes in her book. "But you're not going to be able to convince the scientific community of any of this if you don't have hard evidence to back it up."

Jane was about to reply when there was a rap at the door. All three looked up and their jaws dropped. Standing outside were three of the biggest men they had ever seen and a beautiful woman who held a shield in her hand.

Turning, Thor's eyes widened in delight. "My friends!" he cried, rushing over to let the group in.

The first to enter was the widest of the group. He had a long beard, a big belly, and he wore odd armor that looked ancient and futuristic at the same time. From their talk the night before, Jane assumed these were Asgardian warriors come to rescue Thor. The big man's next words confirmed her thoughts.

"Lady Sif and the Warriors Three," he said, his voice jolly. "Surely you've heard tales of Hogun the Grim, Fandral the Dashing, and I, Volstagg the Svelte?"

Jane stifled a laugh while Selvig raised an eyebrow and gave Volstagg's belly a look.

"Perhaps I've put on a little more muscle since I was here last," he said, sounding a bit hurt.

"That would have been a thousand years ago? Northern Europe?" Jane said, looking over at Darcy and Selvig as if to say I told you so.

Volstagg looked thrilled to be remembered. "Exactly!" he said, smiling.

Thor had been oddly quiet since the Warriors Three and Lady Sif had arrived. Now he walked over and put an arm around Volstagg. "My friends," he said, "I've never been happier to see anyone. But you should not have come."

The warrior called Fandral looked confused. "We're here to take you home," he said.

Jane saw the pain flash across Thor's face. He had not told her everything about the events that had brought him to Earth. But he had said that his actions had caused his father, Odin, to banish him and to strip him of his godly powers, making him mortal. Her heart ached for him. She almost stepped forward to reassure him, but she stopped. The Warriors Three and Lady Sif were exchanging confused looks.

Thor rushed to the Warriors Three and Lady Sif and embraced them all. Then, realizing that there was in fact a traitor within Asgard, Thor bid them leave so that they might return to Asgard to protect the royal family.

But fate had other plans for Thor, and his companions. Lightning flashed across the sky, and the distant sound of thunder boomed. But it was not a storm—it was the Bifrost. Something had followed Lady Sif and the Warriors Three to Midgard. Something much more terrifying.

The sky grew even darker and the wind howled, sending trash dancing along the streets and causing people to duck into buildings for shelter. Jane felt the hairs on the back of her neck stand up. She was frightened, but she was determined not to show it, especially not in the face of Asgardian warriors.

"What is it?" she asked.

Thor looked grim. "I don't know," he said sadly. "Perhaps this is another one of Father's lessons that I just don't understand." His eyes suddenly flashed, showing his determination to do the right thing. "Jane, you must leave now."

She shook her head. "What are you going to do?" she asked.

Before he could reply, Volstagg stepped forward. "He's going to fight with us, of course!"

Thor's shoulders sank and he turned back to his friends. "Not today," he said softly. "I'm just a man." Then, as though comfortable with his fate, he added, "You must stop this on your own. I'll stay and help evacuate this town. But we'll need some time."

Volstagg, Fandral, Hogun, and Lady Sif all nodded in understanding. With a salute to the humans—and Thor—they walked out of the lab and into the growing storm.

As soon as they had left, Thor and the others jumped into action. Racing out into the street, Jane began loading people into various vehicles with directions to get as far out of town as possible. At first, some of the townsfolk balked, but when they saw the storm in the distance, they nodded and got in the cars. Meanwhile, Selvig cleared out Isabella's diner and Darcy rushed to the bus station to tell the driver where to go.

Soon, the place was virtually empty, more like a ghost town than ever before. Satisfied they'd gotten everyone out, Jane, Thor, and the others gathered in the back of the lab. They could hear the sounds of battle, and Jane saw Thor flinch as one of his friends let out a shout.

"Last chance," he said, turning to Jane. He couldn't promise they could stay safe if they did not leave now.

"We told you, we're staying," Jane said, her voice filled with determination. There was no way she was going to leave Thor now. Not when she'd just found him.

The devastation continued, and each time one of his friends was hit or hurt, Jane heard Thor let out a groan. He couldn't stand seeing his friends suffer for him. That was not what he wanted, not anymore.

Finally, he couldn't take it any longer. The mortal Thor—not the mighty Warrior of Asgard—would join his friends in battle, and there was nothing that Jane could do about it. This mysterious man had come into her life and turned it upside down, and now he was about to risk his life for her—and for the people of New

Mexico, as well as everyone in the realms of Midgard and Asgard.

Jane smiled as pride swelled within her heart. Deep down, she knew that Thor would survive. He was, after all, mighty.

EPILOGUE

And so it was that after a long and arduous journey, Thor, the Warrior of Asgard, had finally learned his lesson. With the help of the Warriors Three, Lady Sif, and his newfound friends on Earth, especially Jane Foster, the mighty Thor had learned compassion, humility, and patience. And with those traits, he was now ready to rule Asgard with strength and honor.

But the crown was still far from his grasp. First, Thor would have to figure out a way to return home to the realm of Asgard. Then, once there, he would have to find the traitor within the Realm—and make him pay. There was also the Allfather's health to consider. And what of his brother, Loki? Where was he in all of these proceedings? And what of the icy, warring Frost Giants of Jotunheim? There were many questions to be answered and much to be done, and for the first time, Thor knew that he couldn't do it all alone.

Thor would need his friends, both on Midgard and on Asgard. And he would need his hammer, Mjolnir. Only with all of those elements at his side would the Warrior of Asgard truly triumph. Only then would he be able to accept his destiny as the mighty Thor!

--- ✦ ---

There is more to Asgard and
its surrounding realms.

LET THIS BE YOUR GUIDE. . . .

--- ✦ ---

YGGDRASIL, also known as the World Tree. Its massive branches connect the Nine Realms of the cosmos.

THOSE NINE REALMS ARE AS FOLLOWS: Asgard, Vanaheim, Alfheim, and Nidavellir, Midgard, Jotunheim, Svartalheim, Hel, and Muspelheim.

VANAHEIM is where Asgard's sister race, the Vanir, live.

ALFHEIM is home to the light elves.

NIDAVELLIR is home to the dwarves.

JOTUNHEIM, which has always been an enemy of Asgard, is a frozen realm

---

where the Jotuns, or Frost Giants, live.

SVARTALHEIM is populated by the dark elves.

HEL is the realm of the dead.

The oldest of the realms is **MUSPELHEIM**, which is home to the fire demons.

MIDGARD, also known as Earth, is home to the human population. It is distinct in that it is usually not affected by the events that occur on the other eight realms.

ASGARD is home to many powerful and fabled warriors. The inhabitants of Asgard have superhuman strength, possess mystical powers, and their travels to Midgard, or

———————— ✹ ————————

Earth, have given rise to the Norse myths of old.

THE ASGARDIANS

ODIN ALLFATHER is king of Asgard and the mightiest of the Asgardians.

QUEEN FRIGGA is wife to Odin Allfather, and mother to both Thor and Loki. Her greatest attributes are beauty, Asgardian strength, and great patience.

THE MIGHTY THOR is Asgard's greatest warrior, son to Queen Frigga and King Odin Allfather, and brother to the trickster known as Loki. He is Prince of Asgard, and is next in line for the throne.

───────────────── ✦ ─────────────────

Thor's closest friends and most trusted allies are the WARRIORS THREE, LADY SIF, and LOKI.

HOGUN THE GRIM is the most serious of the Warriors Three, while **FANDRAL THE DASHING** thinks quite highly of himself. **VOLSTAGG THE VOLUMINOUS,** on the other hand, would rather have a good meal than worry about looks or battles.

Though not an official member of the Warriors Three, **LADY SIF** is just as fierce. She uses a shield and a double-bladed sword as her weapons of choice, and her unmatched fighting abilities are equal only to her beauty.

───────────────── ✦ ─────────────────

LOKI, the Master of Magic, knows deep down that the throne of Asgard will never belong to him. Often the voice of reason to his brother Thor, Loki is the one who summons Odin to save them, the Warriors Three, and Lady Sif from the grave threats on Jotunheim, though Loki's motives might not always be completely honorable.

THE WORLD OF ASGARD

ODIN'S MAJESTIC PALACE towers high above the peaceful land of Asgard. It is here that the royal family resides. Two large statues of Odin's fallen brothers stand guard outside the throne room, forever watching over the Asgardians.

———— ✵ ————

ODIN'S THRONE is as impressive as
the mighty ruler himself. Made of the finest
gold, it sits in the middle of the throne
room, demanding respect from all who enter.

Aside from being a powerful and wise
ruler, the great Odin Allfather relies on the
following resources: **GUNGNIR**—This is
the mighty spear Odin uses when in battle.
It is filled with the mystical **ODINFORCE**.
SLEIPNIR—Odin's eight-legged steed. A
loyal companion and powerful beast, Sleipnir
allows Odin to travel on land . . . and air.

Odin's rule has lasted thousands of years, and
at various times over the course of his reign,
the Allfather must replenish the Odinforce by

———— ✵ ————

going into the **ODINSLEEP.** Even though the Odinsleep restores his powers, this may take a few weeks, a few months, and in some cases even longer. During this time, Odin is as powerless as a mere mortal from Midgard.

Throughout his reign, Odin has acquired many items of great danger. These objects are kept deep in the heart of the palace, inside the **VAULT**—which is guarded at all times by Asgard's most elite guards.

While there are many dangerous items inside the vault, the **CASKET OF ANCIENT WINTERS** is the most feared. Taken from the realm of Jotunheim by Odin to prevent the Frost Giants from taking over the Nine Realms, it has the power to cause instant and never-ending winter. It is watched over by Odin's most powerful weapon, a metallic monster known only as **THE DESTROYER.**

MJOLNIR is Thor's mighty hammer. Made of a rare metal called uru, which came from a dying star, it can summon lightning, rain, and thunder.

The side of the hammer carries the inscription: "WHOSOEVER HOLDS THIS HAMMER, IF HE BE WORTHY, SHALL POSSESS THE POWER OF THOR."Only the mighty Thor has the ability to lift this great weapon, whose name translates to "THE CRUSHER."

BEYOND ASGARD

Beyond the walls that surround Asgard lies one of the most important places in all of the Nine Realms, **HEIMDALL'S OBSERVATORY**. From inside the domed building, Heimdall, the all-seeing and all-knowing sentry, controls the magical **BIFROST.**

THE BIFROST is how Asgardians travel between various realms. It is also how others can enter into Asgard.

When he places his sword inside the Bifrost control that lies in the middle of the Observatory, Heimdall can aim the

Bifrost at a specific location. It is incredibly powerful, and when the Bifrost opens in another world, such as Midgard, it causes markings at the landing site.

JOTUNHEIM

The realm of Jotunheim was once full of stunning cities built entirely of ice. After Odin took the Casket of Ancient Winters, the once beautiful buildings began to crumble and melt. Now most of the land has floated away in large chunks. The Frost Giants wander the desolate and lonely landscape, angry and thirsting for revenge against Asgard—and their king, Odin Allfather.

---❈---

KING LAUFEY, the leader of Jotunheim, has a secret plan to bring power back to his once powerful realm, and if successful, it will forever change the lives of Thor and Odin.

MIDGARD

Unlike Asgard with its mighty warriors, or Jotunheim with its Frost Giants, or the other realms with their dwarves and demons, Midgard is rather unmagical. Midgard, also known as planet Earth, has long captured the interest of the Asgardians, who have traveled on the Rainbow Bridge to observe this realm. Over the years, those visits have threaded their way into Earth's Norse myths.

---❈---

Many think those stories are nothing but fantasy, but they are in fact true.

HUMANS

Astrophysicist **JANE FOSTER** is one of the first humans Thor meets when he is banished to Midgard. As he struggles to figure out what it means to be human, he often turns to Jane for advice and comfort. Jane works along side **DR. ERIK SELVIG,** a colleague of hers, and her intern, **DARCY LEWIS,** a college student.

After Thor is banished to Earth by King Odin for disobeying his orders, both Jane

Foster and her friends take a special interest in this man from another world. Jane is looking for proof of spacial anomalies, however she is not the only one who is interested in Thor. Several government agents are also looking at him, but for a very different reason.

S.H.I.E.L.D.

S.H.I.E.L.D. stands for Strategic Homeland Intervention Enforcement and Logistics Division. Led by Director **NICK FURY** and his right-hand man, **AGENT COULSON,** S.H.I.E.L.D. agents have access to advanced technology and sophisticated weapons. While striving to protect the United States—and the Earth—they also run the **AVENGERS INITIATIVE**. Coulson feels Thor might be a great asset to this top secret program.

There is much more yet to be learned about the Nine Realms of the cosmos and its inhabitants . . .

BUT THAT IS A LESSON FOR ANOTHER DAY. . . .